THIS IS NOT THE WAY WE CAME IN

by the same author

Oracle
Winter Investments
The Entropy of Hunters
The Game of Kings

THIS IS NOT
THE WAY WE CAME IN:
FLASH FICTIONS
AND A FLASH NOVEL

DARYL SCROGGINS

RAVENNA PRESS
2008

ISBN: 978-0-9822115-1-9
LCCN: 2008940103

Cover Artwork: Elizabeth Perry
Cover Design: Cooper Renner

Ravenna Press books are listed at Bowker Books in Print
and are available to the trade through our primary distributor,
AtlasBooks, a division of BookMasters:
http://www.bookmasters.com/atlasdistribution/index.html
For personal orders or other information, contact the editor at
http://www.ravennapress.com/books
or write to Ravenna Press,
4917 S. Thor St., Spokane, WA 99223.

ACKNOWLEDGMENTS

Most of the fictions in this book originally appeared in: Asylum Annual, Carolina Quarterly, The Chiron Review, *Double Room, elimae, The Fiction Review, The Madison Review, New Growth* and *New Growth II* (anthologies), *Pearl, Quarter After Eight, The Quarterly, Quick Fiction, Salt Hill,* and *SleepingFish*. "Trauma Man" won the *Salt Hill* Flash Fiction Contest. "Prairie Shapes: a Flash Novel" won *Quarter After Eight*'s Prose Contest and was also published in *PP/FF*, edited by Peter Conners. Several fictions also appeared in the earlier collection *Oracle*.

For Rick and Teel

CONTENTS

Part One

Part Two

Part One

The Farmer's Widow

When the marker had been pounded in with a black stone she looked up at ice clouds—thin wisps at the upper edge of blue—and without speaking turned and began to move into the house she had lived in for more than fifty years. Age slowed her, and she pulled the farm in close. The fields returned to an older order, with its blowzy milkweed and Johnson grass. The kitchen garden narrowed and slipped into a ring around the rotting house, so the old woman had little distance to walk for cucumbers and tomatoes, for okra and summer squash. Finally it was a farm of window boxes and barrels, where strawberries bloomed and fruited and potatoes bulged.

The roof sagged, and when a hail storm brought down half the house the widow moved into a single room at the back corner. For drinking water she set out pots beneath roof leaks, and the laden limbs of a pear tree leaned in toward the house. The briars of a running rose crept through the windows and began to occupy the room, arching over the widow's bed from one window to the next, growing over months and years until her world was a leafy bower. The widow was by now thin and humped, but she kept a space clear for the chair she had made from a little box, where she sat and sipped her rosehip tea. She looked so like a startled fledgling, with her tufts of downy hair, the birds began to feed her, and befriended field mice huddled close to warm her on cold nights.

Then one day, when the house was little more than a thicket of pomegranate and rose briar, there came a sound, the sound of a wagon—its traces giving up muted tintinabulations—and a voice, calling out to anybody in the house. When the widow heard it she fell into a quandary. For she knew that by the time she made her way out the speaker would probably be gone. But she had to try, she resolved, and she set about preparing for the journey. She would have to lose weight in order to fit through some tight places in the vine tunnels and board heaps, so she didn't pack much food—just a few beads from blackberries and some mint leaves. She combed her hair with the sharp tines of her fingers and looked into a little shard of mirror. But her sight was so bad she couldn't tell how much of what she saw was simple memory.

And this sent her into another quandary. How did she know she hadn't just remembered the voice she now sought? She thought how odd it would be to undertake a great journey, just in order to walk into her own voice. But she set out anyway—listening in the way a thicket listens at dusk, when birds make little flights without sound.

Wingtips

Virgil was embarrassed for the pair of shoes that lay at the edge of the ditch, and he pretended not to see them for a moment—pitching an aluminum can into his sack and scanning the weeds for others. Finally he paused and rubbed the white bristles on his chin, which stood out against his black skin like the hairs on an old dog's muzzle. It was a cold morning, with ice clouds so high and wispy the blue of the sky seemed to turn and leave them motionless. Virgil adjusted the fold-down ear warmers on his brown vinyl hat, then faced the shoes directly.

"It's not your fault," he said.

"I know, I know—you waiting for what you was made for. You empty. You out here—like somebody leadeth you to lie down by still waters."

Then Virgil backed off a little, not wanting to be pushy. He stood and looked around at the new subdivision of brick houses he was skirting as he followed the road beside weedy creek bottoms. But he was only looking indirectly, rubbing his neck the whole time. It was a neighborhood of lawns that had been rolled out like carpets, with new cars in driveways, boats in sideyards. And it didn't do, Virgil knew, to look like you were looking too closely at anything in particular.

Virgil looked back at the shoes and squatted near them, plucking at tufts of dried grass.

Black wingtips.

Made of the finest and heaviest leather. No scuffs—and shining like they had just been spit on and rag-popped.

Their perfect condition struck Virgil as a bad sign.

"Mercy, you do carry on with your selfs," he said to the shoes. "You somebody's marryin' and buryin' shoes. You been run out from under by some bad goin's-on."

Virgil imagined vague figures moving in darkness—burglars climbing out of windows, adulterers almost caught and running naked with clothes in hand, until something made them think they needed to run faster, lighten the load.

A boat-tailed grackle flapped over so close Virgil could see the circles around its black eyes, the part-opened beak. And the stillness, the quiet in which he had mused was suddenly loud with the sounds of the waking world. A school bus rumbled and squeaked past him, and across the way an electric garage door began to rise. There was no question about it now: he knew he couldn't get hooked up with those perfect shoes, knew he couldn't afford to risk even the close look he had already given them.

Virgil stood quickly, kicked at a matted collection of garbage for a moment, then moved down the road a hundred feet or so before resuming his search for cans. But he couldn't shake the feeling that he had been included in something he wanted no part of. He moved a bit further down and looked about, but the pall that hung over him would not dissolve, in spite of the fierce yellow brightening of the arriving day. His mood made him feel the chill of the air more acutely, though he had set out and collected on many days colder than this. Just tired, he told himself. Just ready for home—where the dog would be waiting, banging its tail against the clapboard wall. Where a few sticks would make the stove glow, and coffee with milk and sugar would warm his hands.

Out of the corner of his eye Virgil noticed that three boys—probably headed for school—had crossed the road back the way he had come. One picked up a great clod of dirt and pitched it into the muddy ditch, while his companions jumped back, hands remaining in the pockets of their jackets.

"Cut it out, shithead!" one of the boys shouted.

Faintly, Virgil heard the laughter of the others. He picked up the pace of his search, not going for cans he would have to dig for or empty of brown water. When he glanced back the boys had stopped. They were looking down, waving two other boys over from across the road for a look.

Virgil looked ahead at the railroad bridge that crossed the road, the tracks his path home. He made for the steep incline of the bridge base he would have to climb to reach the tracks. When he reached it and started to climb he looked back: they were still huddled around the shoes. They were pointing at him. Only when he reached the top, where he had to pause and catch his breath, only when he was pinned against the sky like a rag did the shouting begin.

A Rare Man

So he gets right up in my face like a crazy man with those gray eyes of his—he had me by the shoulders even—and he says real quick, "Do you think a man can stay like he is no matter what they do to him?" Well, I'm not the kind of person who sits by and does nothing when somebody lays hands on him, but this man looked so desperate that my notion to get loose just played out. He was like a man looking for survivors.

While he was holding me at the shoulders, he turned and looked across the street where there was nothing but a row of foundations the builders hadn't got to yet, and back of that nothing but an old corn field gone to weeds. And I could tell I may as well have been a wall he was leaning on.

He says, "Jesus, that man could lay shingles. Never saw a man yet white or black could do it like him—real steady but fast. He'd pick up a shake, give it three quick whacks, and pick up another like he was spreading butter on his bread. Drank his iced tea like that too—real calm and steady—like none of the coolness was getting away from him. And that time Lewis and James got in a fight and Lewis pulled a knife?"

He looked at me like I really might remember something I never saw.

"And he reached in there real smooth but fast, said, 'You don't need that,' and got that knife, walked back over to the ladder and went back to work. They didn't even want to fight anymore after that, they just put their hats back on and went about their business."

He made a pretty-as-you-please gesture that fell off to his side.

"They came after him today and he went right along with them, let them put the cuffs on him and everything. Deputy wouldn't tell me anything, just said I'd better look for another hand."

He looked up at the rooftops for a minute and then gave me a little clap on the arm. He was almost to his truck, his big shoes making tread marks in the sand where the driveway was going in, before I said, "Yes." He stopped for a second before he remembered he'd asked me a question. Then he gave a little nod and went on.

I could tell right away maybe I shouldn't have said anything. Hell, what do I know, I just pick up what's left when they finish building these things.

But right after he left I picked up a piece of brickbat and threw it all the way across the yard. Went right in the barrel I was using without touching the sides. And I thought, what if I could make it like that every time? What if I was so regular with it I didn't even take notice anymore, didn't just do it because somebody was looking?

I guess it's a rare man can throw like that.

The Painter's Wife: A Letter

Dear Will,

You have not been well for a long time. It started gradually: I watched you forget the names of the flowers you planted for me—cosmos, verbena, periwinkle. Then I saw you stand with your head tilted as if listening, puzzled by the mystery of a comb or a cup—wondering what they could be for. Then I came home to find you bleeding; I had to work, Will, I couldn't stay with you always. I came home to see you slicing at a picture of an apple in a magazine, the knife cutting your hand more often than the picture. "Red," you said, triumphantly.

I am not so young or well myself now, Will. So I can't do for you what others can. I hope to see you as often as I am able.

Will, I don't want a new life, I want the old one. I want to hear you stepping quietly so as not to wake me as you go downstairs to make coffee and to walk the dog. I want you to touch my hair again. I want to hear you say, as the new day floods the windows, "My, my—look at the light"—the room brimming with the glow of your face.

They say it won't happen, that it can't happen, but Will, if you should ever awaken in the night and wonder where you are, if you should wonder where I am and what has become of all you suddenly know again, the nurses will give you this letter as I have asked them to. Read it and then ask them to call me. And I will come out of my wilderness as you have come out of yours, and the world will be ours again.

Always, Dorothy.

Issue From The Grotto Of The Street Hermit Saint

Every night she sat until morning in the high storeroom
of Grace Mercy Church, working at the job she had
made for herself. The minister allowed this, and she
was beholden to him, so she worked by candlelight
to save electricity. And to save candles she used only
one at a time, affixing it at ladder height to a chain
that dropped from a distant ceiling. Its light wavered,
like light reflected from water, above dusty stacks of
folding chairs and a boxed nativity scene, above the
massive desk of carved wood where she sewed the tiny
clothes for the dolls she sold. A vast space lay before
her where she might have spread her work, but she
chose instead to lean over the thin-bottomed drawer
she pulled out—almost to its falling point—from the
desk's ornate front. So dim was the light, a ghostly
visitor floating above would have hardly been able to
tell what task the old woman had taken up. For it was
not so much by sight but by feel that her work took
shape: in darkness there was a close pinching of the
thumbs, a pleating of some thick brocade, and the stab
and glide of thread as coarse as fishline. The pleating
went round and round, as the woman's thick, yellow
thumbnail pressed, folded and pierced, pressed, folded
and pierced, until her back straightened a bit and

light caught the pink plastic of the little doll, its bare arms raised above its featureless bust in a somnolent benediction, its legs glued at pointed toes to a little lacquer stand, and, in between, the brown ballerina dress with its tight spiral of pleats.

The doll she held was one of a countless number, and the slight pause she allowed herself at its completion was one of habit. But this time, for no reason, the pause was longer. For a moment she looked at the doll's pink, waxy flesh, the flashings from the hot mold still untrimmed. And although it was still dark outside, the old woman looked up through the window at her side and imagined how it would look in a few hours—a frame of gray stone reflecting only the blue of the sky, the emptiest of blues, maybe dashed once by a white-brown pigeon, but then reformed whole. What color was that blue, she asked herself, covering her mouth with three fingers. It was the blue of a popsicle she was given once. She smiled faintly. What flavor was it? Coconut? No, no—it couldn't have been that. She waved the thought away.

But an idleness had crept into her work, like the first light of false dawn. The old woman picked up a little comb and rasped it through the doll's auburn nylon hair. With wandering attention she noticed that the comb handle had whorls etched on it, like those on a tortoise's back, whorls like so many threads turned in upon themselves in falling circles—like a song caught in a room—each cell alone among many and bound by a sadness, like having to pick up without a word and move to another city, another kind of weather.

She set the comb down amid an emptiness that only a mildly spiteful idleness can assuage, as if she felt some doleful watcher was appraising her actions, but she didn't care. She poked at the bits of lace and the sheerest scraps of nylon fabric that lay in the bottom of the drawer. She joined them lazily with a tweezing of her horny nails gone suddenly delicate with a gentle effort, and took a stitch here and there with the thread of her own gray hair and the needle with the smallest eye. She toyed with filaments almost lost in the dust and grain of the wood beneath the feet of the ballerina doll. She worked, not knowing what she made, and finally not trying to know.

When gray-blue light filled the back of the room, she rose in the slow stages her back allowed and walked to the window and looked out. The night lights about the city were weak. After a while she looked down at the bit of fluff in her hand, vaguely puzzled by it, and amused. It was shaped like the little bell of a petticoat, with diaphanous waves fluttering down from its center. And the gray threads that held it sparkled like ocean spume.

The old woman turned the crank on the jalousie window. It resisted, leaded with soot and grit, but finally gave and opened, allowing a damp wash of morning air to spill in. She felt the fabric flutter in her hand. She put her arm out as far as it would go, and with two fingers—released. For an instant she thought it would simply drop with as little resistance as any scrap that falls. But it took the blue air and billowed— it sank and rose again, fluttering like a shining medusa with all the ailing lights of the city compounded and scintillating within it, and it drifted outward, but not down, and finally was lost from sight.

She rubbed her hands together and then cranked the window shut, vaguely embarrassed by her deed, but not willing to think about it long enough to admit it—long enough to be reminded again of foolishness, and of work gone to the wind.

Deal

I had a roll put out for Carl, and some coffee, but he didn't come down. Directly I said up the stairs, "Carl, you up?" Most times if he has slept through the alarm I hear his feet hit the floor, and then the water going in the bathroom. All I heard, though, was some sparrows flying in and out under the eaves. I called to him again. Halfway up the stairs, I stopped to listen. "Carl?" I said. Then I came back down.

His truck was still in the driveway. The dog was still in the back yard, looking through the fence at kids walking to school. I went back in the kitchen and put the sweet roll back in the box in the refrigerator. I poured the coffee out. Rinsed the pot. I washed some clean dishes, and when that was done I sorted some laundry. I emptied the washer of towels and took them out to the clothesline. I looked at how much air there is between most things you can see.

Then I went back in and put some fresh coffee on. I got a roll out of the refrigerator, put it on a plate and set it on the table. But I picked the plate up again after a minute and put the roll in a pan. Spread some margarine on it and put it in the oven. When it was warmed, I poured a cup of coffee and put everything on the table. I went to the stairs. "Carl, you up?" I said.

An Opportunity

"Get them," the blonde child commands from the wide porch, and the *criada* waves the butterfly net at the yellow sulfurs. The butterflies are bouncing above ornamental cabbages like little girls in party dresses, dancing at a fiesta, and the maid makes a mere show of catching them.

"There!" the little boy says, pointing. "Get it!" The maid laughs and shakes her head in apology, and she waves on in the same way.

"You're not even trying!" the child says, banging the screen wire bug box against his leg.

So she laughs again and nets a butterfly, careful not to injure it. "*Abra la puerta*," she says.

"What?"

"The door," she says, "open the little door."

The boy works at the latch and steps forward, into the sunlight. The maid opens the fabric before him. She holds the net several inches away from the open door as the butterfly walks to the round lip. It opens and closes its wings twice. And then it flies into the box.

Planning for the Future

We pass a shoe in the road. And then another, but not the same kind. Then a plaid shirt. A mile down, balled socks and a baby blanket.

Ellen says, "I want to go back. I forgot something. I know there's something I didn't—"

"You're just tired," I say.

A pair of dark slacks, ironed to the pavement, flash by.

"I'll stop here at the rest stop," I say. "You can sit for a minute." The air coming in off the desert is fresh. Not much dust in the morning.

A chain link fence separates the rest area from more land that is the same. It has caught a plastic laundry basket like a tumbleweed, and wind holds a family of laundry against wire. A pale blue dress seems to be reaching for the crooked arm of a jacket.

"I can't go any farther," Ellen says. "I don't know why I thought this was the thing to do."

"For Christ's sake, Ellen. We have come this far and it's only a few more miles we have to go." I open her door and stand by it. But she isn't ready to go yet.

While I smoke she folds the clothes. Pulls them away

from the wind's hold, tucking and smoothing. And she stacks them in the basket.

Then she puts the basket on an empty picnic table and we get back on the highway.

Inscription

It was want of something lasting that led her, a young woman, to the gloom of antique shops. Her husband, out front, sat smoking on a bench that had once had a park around it but now faced only a highway loud with passing trucks.

Inside, she came upon a horse carved of dark wood and picked it up. The size of a young cat, it was lying as a cat does, head up—watching all while showing no concern for what might be near. The woman was about to set the horse down when she noticed that one of its ears seemed to be loose. That's all I need, she thought. Somebody thinking I broke it. She twisted the ear slightly and pressed down on it, thinking that she might improve its hold, and as she did so a rolled piece of paper appeared at the horse's mouth. The woman pulled it out and spread the paper against her palm. The whole sheet was the size of a large postage stamp, and a message was written on it in graying ink. She held it to the light of the front window and squinted.

With my hands I made this,
and now these hands are gone.
Say now that the sky is still

> *blue, and that fire warms,*
> *and that green weeds scythed*
> *give up a green smell. Say that*
> *a woman's laughter in candlelight*
> *brings knowledge of waterfalls,*
> *and of snow falling from the moon —*
> *and you will have said what I said, and*
> *it will be true again.*

The woman tapped on the window, motioning for her sprawling husband to come in. "What?" he mouthed, making no move to rise. But she knocked and waved more insistently, so he flipped the cigarette away and pushed himself up from the bench.

When he finished reading the note he turned a blank look on his wife and raised an eyebrow. His wife snatched the note back and rolled it up. She pushed it back into the horse's mouth and marveled at the way a tiny, sliding piece of wood snapped back in place, hiding any trace of a break in the carving.

"I want this horse," she said. "I want to buy it no matter how much they want for it."

"Why don't you just keep the piece of paper?" the man asked.

Outside, back in the car, the man offered again to go back inside and get the horse if it meant that much to her. But again she looked away from him. The man shrugged and backed out into the street. "Where to now?" he asked. But she said nothing.

The Return

It was as close as a man can come to knowing what it's like to give birth. I came out of the brown river with the baby and we both worked for air on the bank. Our trip through the storm drain left my clothes in strips and my shoulders raw, but the boy was okay as far as I could see. He looked to be no more than six months old but he was looking at me like a person would after years of war.

"Let's find who you belong to," I said. I didn't look in the direction of the moiling creek where his mother might be; I looked back up toward the bridge I had jumped from—as if she might have been there too, on the other side, and the baby had just slipped from her arms.

I thought at the time I jumped that I had to save the child before he went under the next bridge, but I couldn't save him or me either. We both went into a dark I knew to be the end. And then we were out.

How do you know it's the same life you get back when something like that happens? There are births and rebirths in dreams, and death is there too.

It was the baby being so sure about everything that set me at ease. A dragonfly came and lit on his toe, and he looked at it like it was part of his foot.

I picked him up and pulled us up through tree roots and slick clay to the back lawn of a big house. At a wide back window a woman, lounging in a robe inside, turned and looked when I tapped. She looked like I was there to haunt her.

A Whipping

The boy could not be caught for a whipping—he was that fast. And he laughed! So that tiredness in the pursuer might give way to the amusement that saves face: such sleek diplomacy! Wiry limbs dodging and leaping the lash, until the barrel-chested father pauses to wheeze and cough, belt limp, legs splayed.

Then the boy points at the night sky and says, "God-a-mighty look up yonder Oh you missed it—a falling star gold as pissed hay."

Both look upward—the man longer, only his chest moving in a regular but slowing heave. The boy looks away, picking at a scratch on his elbow— waiting for words he can remember without aid of understanding.

"Why do you do it, boy? Why do you lift the wire for the fox and hand me the gun? Why do you stare at Mama and hold your breath when she's threading a needle? Why do you tell your little sister her room gets bigger at night?"

The boy looks quick, eyes darting, for a way legs might find an out from words.

But then—then the father presses his advantage with a susurrant tongue. "Why do you work at your clothes like a horse trying to rub a saddle off against a tree? Why do you take the muddy way when a dry path makes a bee-line? Why more berries ate than picked?"

So many questions. And it works: the boy is dizzy, gone snoozy under the murmurous inquisition, and the father gathers him up, hoists him to shoulder like a sack of feed. The way home is cool and silent—the triumphant father walking slowly with his captive, the captive stripping leaves from low limbs to fill the hat brim beside him.

The Lost Book

In his travels Jesus met a man who lived in a tree, and for the first time in all the days he could recall he felt no need to speak. The valley was yet in shadow, but the man, way up high, was caught in sunlight. He had rubbed himself with oil and all the parts of him sparkled like the first thing ever known by light. Jesus thought of words to say that one day might have been written in red. But just then the man looked down and smiled, mildly and without pride. And nodding once, Jesus turned back to the goat path he followed and walked on toward the sea.

In a Manner of Speaking

Being tall, I could scarcely be blamed for not knowing what the children were doing. I was always carrying a sandwich on a plate, strolling about in thought as the little ones wormed through cushions and chopped at each other with rubber hatchets.

Then Nippy got sick and the whole house stopped to watch. Nippy the fearless, Nippy the mail-slot-eating Chihuahua, Nippy the patron saint of lost action-figures: Nippy coughed hard and pitched over onto the floor. Then he stretched once and urine spread around him.

I said—It happens, I'll take care of it. And I went for a shoebox. The kids looked at the five-color illustrations in the Bible and then threw the book into the fireplace. I came back in and said—Nippy is being treated by noble vets who live in Patagonia. The kids got out the atlas, threw it in the fireplace. I said—Nippy wanted a change. Nippy was tired. Nippy realized he had forgotten something back where he came from.

The kids had a team meeting without significantly changing their positions. Then Bud, the eldest, was pressed forward by the others. He cupped his armpit and made a series of farting noises. Stalemate, he said. I talked some more but they were finished.

Hey Dwight

Hey Dwight,
   Here's a piece of advice your life depends on:
Don't move and don't touch anything around you until
you finish reading this. Remember that old boyfriend
I had a long time ago who was an Army Ranger and a
demolition expert? Well, we have been back in touch,
and he wired the whole trailer for me in a special
way. Don't do it, Dwight—don't make a rush for the
front door: when you came through it you armed
everything. I bet you want to pee about now, or maybe
something else. But think about it—is it really a good
idea to lift that toilet seat? You're probably getting that
squinty mean smile on your face now. You think I'm
just shitting you. Well here's a sample. See those two
teeny wires coming out beside the telephone? Look out
back where your truck is parked under the shed and
touch those wires together. Did you do it? Whoa! That
C-4 is some powerful stuff, isn't it? A little piece the
size of a golf ball goes up and everything starts to look
like "instructions for assembly" in a foreign language.
   I'm not really the heartless bitch you have
always liked to call me, standing over me with your
belt in your hand. Why, I have even made you a
snack—your favorite: mince meat pie. It's on the

counter just to your left. I swear there's nothing bad in the pie. But just to be on the safe side, you might want to avoid moving the plate it's on.

Why am I doing this? That's something you should think about while you are stuck out here in the middle of nowhere, afraid to move—wondering when big pain might visit. I have a lot of experience with that situation and state of mind. Also, I don't want to feel rushed for a change. I want to get the checking and savings accounts all cleared out, and when the lump-sum distribution comes (to our new P.O.Box) from the retirement fund, I think I might just amble on down to Mexico.

No need to try the telephone—it's dead. But say you're tempted to check. Say you just have to know for sure. Wouldn't it be ironic to get the side of your head blown off by a receiver that had no dial tone?

Sit tight, Sweetie,

Alice

Action

Hoyt was not going to let the black Chevy pickup pull in front of him again, no matter what, but it blasted onto the shoulder and around a gravel truck and did just that. After some quick lane-changes and hair-trigger accelerator-to-brake-to-accelerator motion, Hoyt managed to give a good bash to the black pickup's rear bumper, and to swerve off onto the Frontage Road exit—which made the joy of it all even greater since it was his exit, the exit he took every morning.

But when he looked up at the highway and didn't see his victim, his eyes shot to the rear-view and he saw the truck sliding and fishtailing down the grassy embankment toward him. Both the pickup and the brown Dodge Monaco careened to a stop in front of the Texaco station and both men surged out, knowing with a panicky kind of glee that it was kick-ass time, and a fine morning for it. Hoyt sized up the other man, checking for any sign of a weapon, speculating in an instant as to whether or not body bulk was muscle or flab. An embroidered name tag on the man's workshirt read "Wayne." Hoyt was wondering if there would be words, or just a lunge or a kick, when heavy machine gun fire split the air.

"What the fuck?" Wayne said. Both men dived

for cover behind some plastic shrubs and now looked at each other—open mouthed and inches apart—as if an explanation was due.

The machine gun dumped a few rounds into a station wagon at the edge of the station drive and a woman screamed. When the ringing in their ears subsided, Hoyt and Wayne could hear her sniveling; she had her back to the rear wheel of the car, on the side that faced away from the station. Wayne stuck his head up, squinting. He cupped a hand around his mouth and hollered. "Hey, junior, what the hell are you doing in there?"

Junior, the station attendant, called out from behind the machine gun, which was mounted on a bolted-down desk in the station office just behind an open sliding glass window.

"Got people trying to get off without paying again," Junior said. "Self serve don't mean free."

"Listen," Hoyt called out, "why don't you just let us get on to work?"

"Stay put. I need witnesses when the sheriff gets here."

"But we didn't see a damn thing," Wayne yelled.

After a minute Junior said, "Well, how do I know that?"

The woman peeked around at Hoyt and Wayne. Her tall hairdo had shifted to one side and her mascara was smeared. She smiled at them, then put her hand to her chest, horrified.

"My baby!" she cried. "I'm going to die here apart from my baby!"

Hoyt and Wayne glanced quickly in all directions.

"Where? Where's your baby?" Hoyt asked.

"Oh, she's not here," the woman laughed, "she's in Lubbock with her grandparents. I got a picture here—see?" The woman held up an open wallet, but it was too far away for the two men to make anything out.

Everybody looked around when the sheriff's big Plymouth Fury eased off of the highway and cruised up slowly onto the station drive. The sheriff sat in the car for a few moments, fooling with some papers on a clipboard. The car's air-conditioner compressor clicked on, increasing the engine idle, which dropped back to normal when clicked off. Finally, the sheriff picked up his hat, stepped out of the car, and adjusted his trousers at the crotch.

"That's the one over there, Clovis," Junior called out to the sheriff. "Over behind that station wagon. Twelve dollars and eighty cents unleaded."

The sheriff nodded, put on his hat and strolled over to the woman, who got up when she saw Hoyt and Wayne stand and dust themselves off.

The woman introduced herself and explained that she had so many things on her mind that she had just forgotten to pay. She pointed at Hoyt and Wayne and said they could vouch for that, and they said yes, they could. The sheriff dumped the woman's purse out on the hood of her car and looked through everything. Finally he said, "Well, you pay Junior his money and we'll let it go this time."

Hoyt and Wayne used the station telephone to call in sick, then both headed over to Dub's lounge. They had to wait in the parking lot for two hours before the place opened, and while they waited they found that they shared several kinds of experience and opinions. Both men had seen action in the Marines, and both ranked football above baseball and basketball.

Hoyt had once seen a freight train hit a meat truck at a railroad crossing, and Wayne had seen a load of tractor tires shift on the back of a semi and break loose on the highway. The longest roller had made it across a bridge and all the way into the next county.

After a few beers, Hoyt and Wayne played a few games of eight-ball, then had a few more beers. In the gloom of the lounge they grew quiet. They pondered the fact that you could just never predict what was going to happen soon enough to see it coming.

Soon the afternoon crowd began to filter in. Among them were some men from the air-conditioning and refrigeration shop where Wayne worked. One of the men saw Wayne and said, "Feeling better, Wayne? Those menstrual cramps'll get you every time."

Wayne looked at Hoyt and grinned.

Without a word, both went into action.

College Town Diversity

"I have to whup you now," Mama's new husband—Wayne—says, but then Carl, the one from before, steps up and says, "You better go on and set that belt down," and then Wayne says, "Not any business of yours—he's no more yours than mine," and Carl says, "I taken him with me to fish once and I don't allow nobody I fish with to come to harm," and then Billy, my real dad as far as I know, comes in with a pistol that everybody can see right off doesn't even have a cylinder in it and he waves it around in a way that could break his wrist, but then Mama cuts a switch off the pear tree that's big around as your arm and starts whittling the stems off into little points and her eyes are all pointy and she says, "Just like you men to get hysterical over a boy reading a Freudian analysis of Hamlet." And they scatter, all of them, burning rubber and wagging boats and lawn mower-filled trailers all the way down Harvard Street, and me and Mama go back in to pop some corn.

Trauma Man

There's a picture in an old medical book I call "trauma man"—my wife's a medical librarian—and it shows a man from about four hundred years ago who is right at the point of getting the shit torn out of him by every kind of weapon they had back then. The weird thing is, nobody in particular is on the delivery end of the weapons. There's an arrow starting to bite in, and a spear and an axe and a hacking sword—and a kind of flaming cannon ball and a club with teeth in it. And the naked man is just standing there, getting all of it all at once.

My wife says it's a kind of visual index: If this happens, see chapter two; if this happens, see chapter six.... I wait for her to look up from the crossword puzzle she's doing at the reference desk before I ask, "Is there a chapter for what you do if everything hits you at the same time?"

"I don't think so," she says, in the tone she uses when young boys come in asking for books on penis enlargement. "But we have a book that deals with how to straighten out contortionists who have cramped up."

I can see how that might be related, since trying to dodge all of that would surely leave a person in knots.

I remember all of this because that was the day the car fell off the jack with me under it. A neighbor—who later said he took the shrill squeaking of my screams to be the cries of a cat caught in a rat trap—came out and found me. He rushed back into his garage and got the floor jack I should have borrowed. Got me out in no time. It was the oil filter that saved me, since I happened to have set it under a suspension cross member. But I had broken ribs and bruises in the shapes of various engine and transmission parts.

That's when I began to wonder if certain things you look at reach out somehow to condition your fate. I was in the hospital for a few days so I had time to read up on it. I found that there is a long history of pregnant women avoiding the sight of devil images and seeking out images of saints—all in order to keep the baby from getting the wrong impression about life before it even starts.

Gwen, who came in to sit with me when the library closed, heard my new ideas and grimaced. Then she lit into me. "So if you see the president on TV"—she pointed at him; there he was—"do you figure something may happen! Well, lots of things will happen. But plain old cause and effect will kill you faster than a picture will."

"But what if—"

Gwen tried to stop me but I had already sat up suddenly to talk, and a rib punctured my right lung. Again.

They wheeled me out and I closed my eyes so I wouldn't see the stuff laid out for the surgery.

When I got to go home they told me to take it easy. No

heavy lifting. No gymnastics. I wanted to be on the safe side so I did nothing but sit for hours in a chair in the back yard, soaking up the sun. I closed my eyes and turned my face toward the sky, letting the rust color of the blood flowing through my eyelids go alternately dim and bright under swaying tree limbs.

Gwen woke me when she got home and treated my sunburn. I thought that was the end of it.

But then I started to take long walks. It was a get-right-back-on-the-horse-that-threw-you kind of thing. I would walk toward downtown, toward Gwen's library, and she would drive me home.

So I was walking past a sporting goods store when something bright caught my eye. The store was closed but dim lights were on here and there. A flare seemed to have been lit at the back wall of the store. I limped over and cupped my hands around my eyes at a plate glass window. I saw bowling balls and archery equipment. I saw shelves of fishing lures and racks of rifles and shotguns. And over where the ammunition was kept I saw a sign that proclaimed "Black powder and muzzle-loader supplies available here." Just beneath the sign there was a wall socket that must have been the source of power for every display case and promotional sign in the building. It was spitting sparks like a whole box of trick birthday candles lit at once. I closed my eyes just before the train hit me.

I couldn't see but I was being carried. I felt somebody drop one thing and then another on the gurney beside my numb feet. Good, I thought, they got my shoes. But then I started to wonder what was in those shoes.

They say I'm in the medical books, spread over several areas of interest. When I see new doctors now, they always slip and say "Wow" when they get a first look. I still have sight in one eye, but yesterday I saw a kid shooting sparrows with a b-b gun.

Here's the dilemma: should I try to see everything I can now, or should I look at nothing and remember what I have seen more closely? Will looking at what you remember do it to you?

Gwen touches my scars in bed at night, waking me. She always apologizes and tries to laugh it off. But I think she is wondering about the mystery of it all. I think she thinks—without realizing it—that seeing such signs of damage will keep it there—a thing to always be considered from a distance. But I know it doesn't work like that. I just don't know how to not look like I do.

Thanks

Thank you Lord for not letting me get tortured like those other poor sons-of-bitches back in the war. And thank you for not letting me go hungry, all except for that one time, well, that one time spread over a few months, which even so wasn't as bad as those around us had it since we had the hams that we didn't let on to anybody that we had. Lord, thank you for putting me in church bus number two, since bus one is the one that went through the rail and over the cliff on the way to the revival up in Arkansas. Thank you Jesus for letting me get the drop on the Mexican that was stealing my pickup—there wouldn't be pistols if there wasn't a right time to use them. I didn't stand in judgment, I just sent him along to you for you to decide on. Thank you for keeping us all for the most part out of jail and prison. Thank you for the power tools. Lord, thank you for the job with the good company and the disability check. Thank you for keeping us free from storm-like disasters—I mean "free from" as to say pretty much even up, what with the insurance settlement for the hail damage and the one burglarization that didn't turn out to be near such a bad thing as we first thought. Thank you for the way you took care of the situation with Kathie about to leave me for the bull rider. The way you had that bull stomp him in the one place that made him no good to her nor her to him—well, I couldn't have come up with a better plan myself. I mean, of course I couldn't, but you know what I mean to say is it was a miracle, never had any trouble like that from Kathie again. Thank you Lord for keeping murder, rape, and accidental death away, all except for Bobby who drowned in the river. I don't know why he didn't listen better when I told him about suck-holes you can drop off into in shallow water that will take you under without even a chance to holler. I don't know why it was him went under instead of any of those other kids—all of them in the same river. And Lord, I also have questions. Pastor Shank, who is from Luziana and not Texas, as you know, says that most questions fall into the doubt category and are reason to be ashamed. But all I want to know is: Should I leave the retirement account just like it is, or should I go in on that mutual fund thing Ed has been telling me about? Also, what's going to work best for me this deer season—the .30/.30 or the 12 gauge with the rifled slugs? Well, thank you again, Lord, and I'll be talking to you again real soon. Amen.

Easter Story

At the talent show in the middle school cafeteria, a boy shows that he can hold his hands up in surrender and cause them to bleed just by thinking about it. At first there is laughter and derisive moaning from the crowd—a joke gone bad and too long in the telling. Then those in the front row of folding chairs begin to point. They can see the back wall through holes in the boy's palms, and the first screams erupt. The Vice Principal steps forward to chastise the boy for causing such a ruckus, then abruptly ducks into a crouch, scanning the assembly for the silencer-equipped firearm that must have targeted the boy's hands as he raised them for quiet. Teachers usher the children out and search them.

Thus the show ends. And later, when the boy's hands are inspected and found to be whole—absent of any stain or scar—he is punished. Bent over, he gazes into the aquarium in the Vice Principal's office as the board descends again and again. The man is on a mission with a blunt instrument, and he gives himself over to the love of such work. The boy thinks of water and waves; he thinks of the rhythm of pain that is part of the pang felt when something beautiful presents itself to the senses: evening clouds in the moment when they lose flame and pale to ash; the tiny lights fish carry with them into weed caves; the bird's beak still open after the call is finished.

When he raises himself finally, and turns, his face is shining with calm. "Insolent whelp," the man proclaims. And he adds suspension to the boy's punishment, crossing his name off the roll.

Failed Prodigal

The island children will not be still for pictures; he wonders if they know it is a different time he is framing. Lithe girls in fuchsia, and frayed rope boys crumbed with bits of shell.

When they are flitting about like parakeets he calls them over. "Look," he says, holding a magnifying glass to sand, "you are all walking on a field of broken glass."

A dark-haired girl coughs and spits out blood, and a small dog barks at the shape on the sand. The visitor says, "I don't remember, is there a doctor here?" The children point west, to water.

A boat arrives like the color blue failing to hold true. But the dark-haired girl won't come down from the arched tree she has climbed; she hugs the rough trunk and averts her eyes. A medic leaves medicine, but as the boat is leaving the dog rushes in to snatch it up and dash away. After a while the animal returns, distant and distracted, as if beset by a new wisdom or a jumble of names.

Soon the children make a house of sand—a great room like a silo with a low door. They crowd into it, their bodies close as cells in a honeycomb. "Come in," they say. "Quickly!" And the young man joins them.

Beneath the bright flue all wait for revelation, swatting at flies. "Treasure is buried beneath us," a small boy says, "but the island is sailing faster than we can dig." The young man longs then for mimosa blooms, for hawk moths that kiss with a spiraling tongue. He longs for bowls of bright sherbet served at birthday parties on green lawns, and for Chinese lanterns in evening trees.

It is at that moment that the girl comes down from her watch. She says she can see through walls. She says the hidden ones will have to learn how to walk all over again, now that they have lied to the sand about what they are.

Catch Me

After I sold all of my clothes I would sit for big parts of the day in my underwear at the upstairs window, watching as my coat rounded a corner and disappeared, or my red shirt paused in front of the fruit stand.

The rest—everything—I left at the curb for scavengers.

Now light comes into the room and I am polite, I don't disturb it.

The telephone was not mine, but it is gone, too. Perhaps the telephone company is calling me but all the sounds stay in the wire. I made a birdhouse out of the mailbox and put it in the tree at my back window. No nest in it yet. But then, it is autumn.

If you fill a glass with water, if you fill it to the top and then fill it some more, the water bulges above the glass and wobbles. That's the only part I drink.

I have always been pale, but now, in the dark, the whiteness of my underwear seems dim against me. I take it off.

I wonder how long. I wonder how long before someone comes. The electricity is no more, but the water is always there, so ready to fall it will find a way.

I would have thought someone would have

come by now. They will come in and rock me, and brush my hair out of my face. They will dip a finger into something warm and sweet and touch it to my lips. They will rock me and whisper shhhh, even though I have made no sound.

I leave the door unlocked. Not just unlocked, but ajar—there is no need to knock.

Today some people came. I heard their voices and could tell it was two women and a man before they came up the stairs. One of the women talked about how lovely the light was, and the man said some repairs would have to be made. The three of them stopped in the hall outside the door and talked about money, then one of the women, a young woman, walked into the room, followed by the man. They glanced around. I thought they looked right at me, but I guess they didn't see me. The woman said, "Oh." Then she said, "This is not the way we came in." And they retraced their steps.

Down The Rivers Of The Windfall Light

From the Sachitaw, Oklahoma *Daily News*

The body of thirteen-year-old Melissa Bluecrow and that of her prematurely born infant son was found late this morning in a ravine at the west side of town. The bodies were discovered by John Watts, a maintenance worker employed by A & R Radiator Shop, who was dumping garbage in the area. Sheriff Tom Corley reports that the girl's grandmother and guardian, Mrs. Wanita Bluecrow, was unaware of her granddaughter's absence until contacted by authorities. Mrs. Bluecrow was also unaware of the girl's pregnancy, saying only that her granddaughter had complained of abdominal pains early Monday evening and had been sent to bed. The county medical examiner cited "complications due to childbirth" as the cause of death. The child was stillborn....

Birth, and her mouth formed an O. And she remembered, with blood going and going in darkness down her legs, the day of the dog skeleton at water's edge, drinking. And the light! Watermist rising so thick the shadows of fish moved among trees, through bottom land hollows, lingering amid windfalls. Found a milky stone on wet grass—it was the morning fog, clinging to itself! A cold dreamland, caught in a pocket. What had

become of it? She closed her eyes and looked for it—
and she was running because a fear was behind her,
stumbling, almost to this place, panting, falling, and
when she remembered his pulsing, his groaning, she
watched pictures flicker with a strange light through a
little window. There were plums on a cold plate. And
one of them was a dark auto that stole children—that
pulled up in a ravine like an orb of sticky fear. Inside,
flesh was pulled apart like petals—the pollen of
death's odor hovering near—and in the mud a wasp
kneaded a bit of pulp, its mouthparts rippling, its
abdomen bobbing up and down. And she had given
up to a master of pain.

But not before she told herself—Break into me
and I will close my eyes around you, and when you
reach for a hand in darkness you will find my teeth.
And she bit into his screaming and ran. And ran.

She opened her eyes and saw the silent baby,
steaming on the leaves. She closed her eyes again and
dreamed she dozed in moonlight in a canyon full of
broken toys. And in her dream a shadow man came
and took the baby and left something in its place. She
opened her eyes that would no longer focus, to see
what it was—and it was the milky stone, the fog fallen
upon itself, the cold pocket.

It was difficult to see, or to remember to see,
though light was coming. When she smelled it, and
felt it touch her hand, she struggled once and lifted her
eyes. And suddenly, in unison, all the blackbirds rose
as one.

Trouble on the Road

The prisoners were on their way to die when their bus was delayed. Something wrong on the road—a fruit seller gesturing, and a woman loudly giving birth. Panels of silk in sherbet colors billowed, and a carpenter's load of fragrant wood had shifted, spilling. A small boy, wobbling at the task of fetching water, struggled in bare feet across a field of stubble. Goats, looking on, tilted the world to their slant view.

Some cut-throats and thieves were dispatched to help, and soon a report came back of other problems: A farmer's cow was stuck in a pond; A barn roof was being ill repaired by a deaf man; A line of laundry had been blown into a tree; A man's daughter would not come out of his cellar.

The guard behind the wheel shrugged; meals would have to be prepared for the helpers, so a traitor was sent to gather supplies. Prostitutes were let out to build fires. A false priest was released from his shackles and temporarily deputized, his mission limited to requisitioning funds.

The radio, sputtering threats, was answered by the driver with rude hand signals. Others were sent to bring the others back. But soon there was a marriage procession passing, and all paused to watch the local woman and the stranger heading for vows, the new priest leading the way. Only then was it discovered that the rear tires of the bus had been spirited away; the driver stepped out for a look, and when he returned the radio was gone.

Anger filled the man and he took up rifle and sword. He walked the edges of the village, stealing as he went, and he slashed at those who objected—until he was captured. His captors stripped him naked and chained him to a fig tree in the square. Others of his sort were being collected, he was told, and when a large enough group was gathered a bus would be sent for.

Twilight arrives, and children prompt their pet monkeys forward with gifts of oranges. Silent, at the tittering group's edge, a shy girl looks on. Dreaming of escape herself, she gazes at the chained man until darkness takes him.

And then she runs to fetch a saw.

Oracle

"You don't have to sing to know what birds are for."
That's what Mama said, but she's dead now.

I've got others:

"Dark thoughts live in the fire."

"All that's comely might have wently."

That last one was from when she had already gone to live in the home.

She told me once, "Doug, you need to tie a string to what you're about to forget and reel it back in." I wish it was that easy—especially since I'm not young anymore myself. I remember our old address, and it's been torn down. There's no reeling that one back in. It had wood floors and high ceilings. I was about three once and sick in bed. I looked up at a window—a square of blue sky—and when I went to sleep, I dreamed only about that blue square. Some things stay with you.

My wife, Joyce, says that a woman at her work's husband drove home from work and kept driving until he ran out of gas and had to call somebody to come get him. He didn't even know where he was. They tried to say it was some kind of brain problem, but we all knew it was nerves—I mean, my God, the man teaches at a public school.

Now Joyce has started looking at me funny, just because I've taken to writing a diary. She said she never heard of anybody starting a diary by going back fifty years and trying to catch up. But I just think things ought to be complete, and I have a system. I have a notebook for each year, and when I remember something, I simply find the right notebook and write it down. Now, what's strange about that?

I do have two problems, though. I realized the other day that, long before I get all these other notebooks filled, I will have started recording good finds from the past in this year's diary. And since I'll have to say something now about what I remember from then, I'll start to have two entries for everything. This is just asking for confusion.

My other problem has to do with something almost philosophical. I was flipping through one of the notebooks I'd just made an entry in the other day—just fanning the pages real fast without reading anything—and I noticed that a bunch of white pages would flip by, and then a short group of darker pages with writing, then more white, and long or short dark, and more white, and so on and so forth. Now, I wonder: Could this be some kind of bar code? A bar code of life? I scanned through all the notebooks, and it sure looks like one. But I'm still waiting for what it all means to rise up in my mind.

I really don't have anybody to talk to about this. Every time I present an idea of this magnitude to Joyce, she starts to giggle. Now, Mama would have had something insightful to add.

I just know I'm on to something big.

Under Construction, Under Repair

Setting

Horizontal billboards viewed from the air: Letters; pictures.
A landscape of signs spread flat upon a dark forest of
supporting pins. Signs laid out for aerial viewing upon a
snowy plain. A plane of signs—a forest of rods, now that
we are closer to an edge. A forest of poles, with branching
supports—like the underpinnings of a roller coaster, but
dark above. And within—far back in cave-dark—a little
light burning fiercely, where three workmen break for
lunch.

Characters

Chuck: Lead man, mid-forties. Muscular, thinning hair.
Saves pocket change in a jar with hopes of buying a Depth
Master fish finder for his bass boat.

Lewis: In charge when Chuck is sick, early fifties. Never says
much. Sometimes buys a party tray at the deli, stacks all the
folded meats and slices of cheese in his lunch box, and eats
all of it by himself.

Bubba: (Real name: Edward) Brother-in-law to Chuck, which
is the only reason he has the job. Seventeen. Long, blonde
hair and brown doe eyes. Slack hands with slender fingers.

Given to long, meditative pauses and, sometimes, fits—all of which his mother attributes to his having eaten a whole bottle of silver b-b cake decorations when he was two.

*

"Bubba, it's the wind, goddamnit!"

Chuck's sandwich looks like a cloverleaf cookie cutter has been after it, and he wishes Bubba would quit staring moon-faced into the jumbled darkness. He wishes he would knock it off with the dreamy crap and eat something like a regular person would.

Lewis stirs his iced tea with a welding rod and says, "I think he sees something," touching his head so Chuck will see what he means.

Chuck and Lewis chew for a while but then notice that Bubba is crying. Big, silent tears, wiped off now and then with the back of a wrist. Chuck kicks his lunch box closed.

"Jesus, I hate it when you git like this, Bubba. What is it?"

After a few sniffles, Bubba speaks up.

"I think it's something we're under. I think it's this part of the sign we're working on. I think we're working on something that really says something. I think I was born under this letter or word or picture, whatever. I think if I could get up there—get high enough—I could see it. But then, then I could never tell which one it was."

Chuck shakes his head in a slow wag.

"It all leads back to you, doesn't it? The whole fucking business was put here just to make you wonder, wasn't it? Well, why is it all so sad to you, is what I want to know. Don't you ever think we might just be doing some good here? Doing something that points to something not only you but everybody else might benefit from?"

Lewis stands up, pops the dust off his behind with a couple of banjo slaps, and makes ready to get back to work.

"Just wait till next year," he says. "Next year they start laying these signs out on that corrugated stuff that looks like the edge of a cardboard box. Talk about needing a map! Talk about suffocating! But, you won't hear me complaining about it."

Bubba closes his eyes and tries to imagine his sight zooming out from under the darkness—out and up into the sky. He bursts free and ascends. He turns to look down, but finds himself growing dizzy—lost in the graininess of falling snow.

Undertow

I had just said This is Me, This is Not me, I had just been humming that little tune, with wind and sky between verses and a sound like somebody calling me while I couldn't move or speak—I had just said This is not me, when I saw the marble. My cheek was on the ground when I saw the marble half-buried in the dirt. I whispered Marble, but I couldn't stop the dream-thought of an eyeball in sand, watching me. The dream was like looking at all the little lights in soap bubbles— like letting go of everything you see with, letting the bubbles be everything. But this was dirt. Bits of twig. Pebbles. A rusted bottle cap, a bug wing. Root hairs, blowzy dust and sand where small waters went once in rivers—and the eye. Milk glass and blue.

I lie in the dirt, looking, but pretend I don't see. I look at a small shell, but it turns in a circle, faster and faster, and slings me over to the eye.

Then, the shadow of my brother. He sees my hand reach quick to cover the eye, so he won't see. But he pries my hand away—gets a dime out of his pocket and works at the marble with the edge of it. The marble pops out. There's a socket-hole in the dirt.

My dream-seeing moves to the round hole in the dirt, and somebody is asking and asking for the marble. The dream reaches for the peeled grape a brother offers, and there is sand in the eye from looking, looking into the hole in the dirt.

I rock, because Mother is saying A sea once covered the whole state. She is saying Sediment. She is saying Shale, Fossils, Ammonites. When I roll onto my back the blue of the sky curves and I shiver. I am so small I don't stop anywhere. Everything sees everything. Father says We can't afford this. He takes off his belt and says Physical therapy. With each lash, part of a word escapes. Say it, Father says. Say it, Father says. Say it, Father says. When the word comes clean it is two words. Two words I have heard. Fuck you I say and the whipping stops—the whole family grinning in the evening light, their teeth showing—each its own death speaking.

Not This Way

I don't like stories in which a person "fingers" fabrics or "pads" into the kitchen for more tea. I don't like to hear that a person has "stormed in" or "stormed out," even if it has something to do with the fabric or the tea or suburban drama—or the fact that, afterwards, "nothing will ever be the same." I don't like to encounter the words, "In the first place" at the beginning of a sentence, and I don't want to hear that a person turns a "quizzical" expression upon another person. No "chagrin." None of this is bearable, even if it's the police who are nonplused as they look at the cloth the woman is strangled with, and the spilled tea, and the mysterious signs of no forced entry. I don't want to hear that the pregnant woman was a policeman's wife. And please, avoid the interjection of a face peeping in at the open front door, a neighbor's face (the whole world descriptively behind her), a person who starts by saying, "I'm sure it's nothing, but…." Best at this point would be a burst of intricately mumbled confession and the bare beginning of a general realization. After that I would be happiest if one of the detectives just shot the neighbor, then his partner, and then the yapping dog. I would be happy if he just left the damn gun on the table.

Fortune Teller's Stroke

My future killed her. Or was it what I asked her? I asked her which farm my dog had been sent to live on, and maybe she wasn't good with kids or dogs or farms. But she took a breath like winter at the window and all the tarot cards popped up tumbling. Then the mostly skin cancer husband came in from the living room with the parakeet on his shoulder and checked her pulse at the throat.

I let myself out through the screen door. The ambulance passed me on my way home. And that's when Shep ran up to me, wagging. Mama was more surprised than I was. "Must'a been some other dead dog we found," she said. Then she caught herself and said, "I mean that went to work with sheep."

Somehow it all seemed like a kind of trade to me. But then the crying at the funeral made me wonder at the price. A deal made in a dream, and debt stretching out well past any dog's days.

Diamond Solitaire

The boy slides the ring onto the girl's finger, and she holds her hand up in a ray of sunlight. Only then do they see the flaw—an inclusion that suggests the shape of a person falling from a great height toward the brilliant cut stone's bottom point. It is a flaw so large as to account for how such a large diamond could have been bought for so little, though the down payment was close to all there was.

They gaze at the gem, each facet-flash a day linked to others by dizziness, like the slow flicker of bees about a flowering shrub. And behind all there is a constant sound, as of wind crossing a taut wire above an open plain.

Later, at the pawn shop, the jeweler removes his loupe and looks up, wordless for a moment, and tired, as if he's seen it all.

Parting

"Quick—a story! The bus is leaving!" she said. And so it was: the air brakes released like my will to stand gone faint. But I trotted along beside the open slash of window, into the wet street. I worked at the idea for a story as I ran faster. It would have to be good, and it would have to matter. I was on the verge of something when the bus got its second wind, suddenly, and I knew that the chorus of its pistons would rise above me. All I could do was position myself in the middle of the street, in newly-aged September light—hoping to be framed squarely by the back window of the bus. A small figure, with story.

Part Two

Prairie Shapes: a Flash Novel

Prairie Shapes: a Flash Novel

1.

Of the many trails leading west, one that was seldom used crossed an expanse of prairie surrounded by mountains on all sides. A pass on the eastern rim allowed entry, and another, almost straight across to the west, was the only exit. The grassland of the great bowl bulged and sagged in places, but only gradually. This led to the effect, experienced by drivers of the wagons that occasionally labored through, of an always ambiguous horizon. The sky became more definite than the land, in spite of clouds that sometimes crossed it quickly and sometimes lingered to keep pace with a cart drawn by oxen.

It was easy for people crossing this prairie to believe that they were being judged by silence. It was as if their actions were being viewed, even when night found them under buckboard and blankets, hidden from the gritty light of stars so profuse as to magnify every kind of distance known to humankind. Always there was the sense that either nothing would happen—ever—besides wandering, or that the world would be destroyed in an instant by a comet or some infinite collapse of the ground.

The only structure in the whole prairie was a small house made of clay. Its red walls were the same color as the road beside it, and it lay at the midway point between the passes. The house was built so close to the road that a baby, in his crib by a window facing the trail, could put a hand out and touch the damp flanks of the horses as they passed. Morning-glories bloomed around the window, and the baby's eyes were blue—so those who looked in as they passed often didn't see him there.

His mother made her living replenishing water barrels from a well so deep that the man who dug it was said to have never come back up. The woman generally lowered the bucket only when the baby was sleeping, unless reliable travelers were present to watch after him as she worked.

But one autumn morning the woman awoke with a fever that didn't allow her to escape her dreams. She rose from her bed with the black dress she slept in smoking in the cold air, and she scrawled a note in chalk on a slate. Wracked with chills, her hand shook as she wrote: Please watch the baby, dear traveler—I must find warmth or all will be lost. She propped the slate on a table by the door and fled.

A lone traveler, a man moving on foot in the rarest of directions—west to east—was the first to arrive, and he could not read. The man waited for four days, feeding and comforting the baby—watching for some parent or guardian to return. But one day was the same as the next. Finally, he took up the slate and wiped it clean with a dishcloth. He looked at the blank surface for a long time. He could not write so he drew pictures and symbols he hoped would show that the baby was safe and would be returned. Then he packed what he could find of the baby's things, and wrapping the child in a blanket he resumed his journey.

2.

The woman reached the southern mountain rim with blistered feet and her face chapped by wind. But she did not stop at the imposing wall. She turned abruptly to the right and then about face to the left. Her pacing lengthened with each cycle of turns, as if the dog's habit of circling for a trail had been adopted but flattened into a line. At the end of one cycle, just as she was about to reverse course, she saw the edge of a canyon that led further south. She turned into it and went on. She followed its rocky edge to the point at which the wall across from her drew near and merged with hers in a dead end. With little room to move, her pacing became a kind of davening. And then she began to climb.

She had only scrabbled up a few feet when she found the mouth of a small cave. She looked in, and seeing light she headed toward it straightaway.

It was a tight fit on all sides. The woman pressed forward, tearing her clothes and cutting her hands on sharp stones. Ahead the passage seemed to open upon a larger realm, but the tunnel narrowed so severely at that point that she had to expel all air from her lungs while pushing forward to reach it. For a moment she was stuck and dark spots crossed her field of vision.

But she pushed with the last of her strength. She felt her clothes and the skin beneath them shred, but breath came again as she tumbled into a dim chamber.

For many minutes she lay on her back, taking in great draughts of air—feeling it sluice into her blood, cooling her. When she opened her eyes she knew that she had been feverish, and that her fever had broken.

But an odd view presented itself to her. She was on her back and the light she had taken to be a way through the mountain was now above her. The woman sat up and saw the trick that had beguiled her. At her feet lay a glassy pool of water, and above light fell as if through the top of the tallest of chimneys. Light, striking the pool, rebounded to reflect off a wall of quartz. So the way through—or out—was impossibly high, or back the way she had come.

In a panic the woman's thoughts turned to her child, and she wondered how long she had been gone. She saw in her mind the sharp face of a fox that had watched her on her way south. And she saw the child standing in his crib, waiting.

The woman pulled herself back to her point of entry, and only then did she see that the chamber she was in was a geode. Crystals grew in sharp spikes from the walls on all sides, and like the spines in a pitcher plant they lined the edges of the tunnel she had passed through. When she had torn wide grooves in her shoulders without even beginning to fit herself back through the opening, she sat by the pool, rocking. She watched the beam of light arc wide across the wall and finally chase itself out the top of the world. And she knew she would have to become smaller before she could escape.

3.

Dogs barked as the man turned toward the farm's gate, the baby boy sleeping in the pack on his back. He walked up the lane past roses on fence rails, to find his wife waiting on the wide porch. She said nothing, long after he was in hailing distance, and seeing that she made no move toward him the man hung his head.

At last he stood and looked up into her face. Two years away. He wondered when the turning point was, when he had begun to think of nothing but return.

But his wife seemed as tired as he. And he saw then the worn path in the wood of the porch floor, the missing paint, the raised grain of the planks where she had turned, and turned.

She rubbed her hands on her apron, which meant she had already prepared a meal for him. They went in, to table. The boy awoke when the man swung his pack from his shoulders. The man was about to explain when he saw his wife's face as she saw the child. She looked from the child to her husband, and back to the child again, and the man saw in her face more excitement and love than he had ever known her to have. It was as if his failure in the West and the long months she spent tending the farm alone had been erased.

His sleeping wife held the hand of the sleeping boy, and in the dark the man thought of the little clay house in the middle of the prairie. He built stories for himself of the certain death the boy's parents must have met to have left him where cold or the boldest of wolves could have ended all quickly. And he slept then, as a man with a family again.

4.

The woman touched her tongue to water but would not drink. Ten times the light had crossed her retinal room. She passed the time by singing, directing her voice toward the window above her with hopes that her child might hear and be soothed.

She rose, finally, her wounds crusted over, and removed the last of her clothes. She slicked her body with silt from the pool. When she tried the tunnel again her wounds were reopened, but this time her shoulders slid through to a slightly wider space. Only thoughts of her child allowed her to press on against pain, until her hips were free of the edge and she was crawling again toward light.

A full moon showed her the emptiness of the house long before she reached it. She walked faster, panting, and reached for matches as she tumbled through the open door. All empty, and dust on the baby's sheet. She lit a lantern then and saw the slate. At the left side she found a stick figure of a man, with hat and rifle, walking. Then a small drawing of a baby. Then a tall box with a door on it and a dial with numbers—a safe. And finally an arrow, pointing at the safe.

The woman considered the drawings for only

a moment before reaching for clothes. She picked up a tin of biscuits and a canteen and struggled to dress herself as she set out—headed west to find the man who, no doubt seeking his fortune as so many did, had left with hers.

5.

The boy grew. His new father showed him the needs of cows and chickens and the subtle weaknesses of fruits and vegetables. And the boy seemed inordinately—wonderfully—avid to learn such things. His mother marveled at the boy's caring ways; but she worried about the way he seemed always to be musing. Often she saw him standing, when his chores were done, in an uncultivated field, swaying with the wind as if he might float away like the milkweed seeds billowing around him. The same look came to his face when his father spoke of his travels west. Always he asked for stories of the open plains and of mountains, and when the tales moved on to cities and forests, the boy seemed to have stayed behind, lingering, waiting.

6.

A city loomed, and the woman made her way through it as if she had set a whole marsh of birds aflight while hoping not to do just that. Everywhere she asked if a man had passed through with a child, but people shied from her, crossing the street to avoid her. A glance in reflecting window glass showed her a gaunt, shambling figure who appeared to have climbed from a grave. She sold the necklace she found around her neck, and found a secondhand dress and a place to bathe. She was then able to ask her question everywhere, but still without result.

A week passed, and she was taken to a doctor when she collapsed in the street. The man's face was stern and distracted as he fed her soup.

"What can you do?" he asked.

"What?"

"Abilities. In what way might you make yourself useful?"

Through several spoons of soup the woman thought about how she might answer.

"I can draw water," she said.

"Ah, an artist." The doctor's mouth twitched upward for an instant, then went back to its straight line.

*

She worked for the doctor, doing the things he showed her how to do: checking bandages, cleaning instruments and floors. She slept in the room behind his office, and when she was not needed she took her question out into the city by the ocean.

A man said—Yes. Said he thought he knew the person she was seeking. He had seen a man and child who appeared suddenly and kept to themselves in a shack near the wharf.

But when she found the place the man was drunk on the dirt floor, propped against a wall, and the child was a girl. The toddler looked up at the woman and raised both arms toward her. And the woman took the child up in her arms. She left a note with the address of the doctor's office written on it, but the drunk man never appeared. When she went back the next day the man was gone.

7.

The boy did well in school. He learned to read and in his practice at the kitchen table he taught his father to read. A rich woman in town started a lending library, and the boy brought home books of poems and books filled with pictures of machines and distant lands. Geography was his favorite subject, and he found places on maps that seemed to him forlorn for lack of roads and towns. He wondered what grew there— what the soil looked like.

The boy's mother smiled when he read poems to her. She told him one day that his voice moved like wind in a field of tall grass, but just then she coughed into her hand and bright blood trickled down her forearm.

He read then of medicine, seeking knowledge as if he hoped to gather years of study in the course of each long evening. In the end, though, when he was almost a man, he came home from the library to find his mother still, on her bed, and his father digging just beyond the garden.

The boy stood by his father for a while, then went back in to cook some supper. When he went back out at dusk his father was below ground and still digging. The man looked up and asked for a lantern.

"Don't heat the house," he said, "this could take a while." It was late October and the nights were already cold. The son worked the farm and lowered food to his father, who seldom spoke and ate little.

Then one day he heard a clanging sound coming from the grave. It was noon and his father was illuminated in the hole far below. He had reached a shelf of rock and was banging at it with a maul. The boy marveled at his father's unflagging energy and feared the man's heart would burst before the stone did. But just then the maul gave up its ringing for a dull sound, and on the next strike a section of rock gave way and fell. It dropped through a space of a few feet into a gray blur of rushing water. The father looked down, standing at the edge of the hole, and made no move to catch the ladder as it slid into the water, its whole length going under before it rose again part way, swung flat, and slipped away.

The son lowered a rope and his father climbed it; he reached the surface and was instantly striding toward the barn. There he gathered his tools and pulled out the fine wood he had been saving for furniture he wanted to build for his wife. He built a coffin for her of cherry and bird's-eye maple.

The boy woke when the sound of woodworking stopped. But how long ago had it stopped? He saw that his mother's body was gone and he ran to the grave's edge. Far below his father squatted at the edge of the hole. He was leaning down, holding the prow of the boat-box with his fingers, looking at the woman's face for the last time. He released his hold and the box entered the dark. The boy could not tell, then, if his father slipped or dove, but in an instant the hole was empty but for the hole within that opened upon a river.

8.

The woman still looked for her boy when her work was done, taking the little girl with her. But as the child grew the searching became a habit of strolls and picnics. They went to street markets and brought fruit. They listened to music played in parks and browsed in old shops where all was covered in dust. In one such shop the woman bought a box of watercolors and brushes for the girl. Back home, in their small room, the child took up a brush and began painting as if painting were seeing. It made the woman dizzy to see places unfolding at such a rate. She watched the girl work as if gazing out the window of a moving train. When the last sheet had been torn from the tablet and filled, the woman was seized by a claustrophobia that sent her out into the alley gasping for air.

"I'm sorry, the child said, "so sorry—I won't do that again."

The woman looked at her then with a fierce concentration, and taking her hand she walked in a half-run to a stationers, where she used her week's money to buy paper. She bought a great roll of paper— a roll so large that a clerk from the shop was sent to carry it for her. She gave him lemonade when he had set his load down and he drank two full glasses before putting his hat back on to leave. But as he turned to go he noticed the paintings strewn about one side of the room.

"You an artist?" he asked.

The woman smiled and pointed at the child, who hid her face behind her hands.

"Mercy," the boy said. "She could paint scenes on walls in restaurants and theaters anywhere."

9.

The boy sold the cow and the mules. He sold the hogs and gave the chickens to his closest neighbor, a widow who lived in a house caved in on one side from rot. Then he nailed the barn door shut and boarded up the windows of the house. Of his parents' things he took only a few mementoes, and a few items likely to be useful: his father's clasp knife—with its blade almost gone from sharpening—and a pair of trousers and a coat that fit with only a slight scarecrow effect. And he took his mother's necklace.

When he had boarded up the front and back doors, he took a canteen and walked to the grave-well. He lowered the container on a cord until it touched the rushing water and was filled. He drank. The water tasted of stone and metal—and the taste made the boy think of moonlight.

He set out, heading generally west, with the thought that work along the way would suggest a course.

10.

The woman was sick, but she hid it so that even the old doctor she worked for didn't notice. She didn't want the accumulating proceeds of her daughter's painting to be squandered on cures.

She began to watch the world as if from a distance, much as her daughter did when she painted. She came to think that she might watch so quietly from her window as to finally see all she had wanted to see. Streets dropped below her toward the waterfront, and people passed in droves and in trickles. Sometimes they walked alone, their movement a mirror of the motions of crowds. People went in to escape the weather, and came back out when storms passed—like gulls retreating from waves and rushing back again to new washed sand.

Once she saw a boy walking. She knew he couldn't be hers, since hers would be a young man now. But she closed her eyes and imagined herself running down to him, holding him. When she opened her eyes the boy was gone.

The woman rose to set about her work, but sat down again quickly with a pain in her chest. She remembered then how her daughter had once exhausted the little pats of color in her paint box, and had painted on with only water. Blue and gray images unfolded, as if scenes from a land of summer were set in snow.

11.

The land the girl painted lay to the east, wistful patrons said. She had begun to lose commissioned work on murals because of a new sadness that had entered her work. A blankness of sky and landscape in her painting rose through even the most precise and artful details. Her employers couldn't say exactly what was different in her efforts—only that it now left them wondering about all they would never live long enough to see.

The girl was not disturbed by these developments; there was little reason to continue her paid work since she had discovered the money her mother saved for her. She wondered how they had managed to live with so much of what they earned being set aside. And she found the notebook in which her mother, already sick, had put down brief glimpses of her days in a small house in the middle of a plain. The girl read and heard in her mother's words the sound of wind in grass. Words combed out in a rhythm as soothing to her as the memory of being rocked in a rocking chair.

She headed east, believing that an ocean would stop her, wherever it might appear.

12.

The boy followed a map his father had made for him in the blank end pages of a children's book, and along the way he read the book again—tales of children adventuring in a wild land, protected by abundant luck and hints of a capricious providence. Rain sent him into an uninhabited hunter's cabin, and he settled into the quiet of it so fully as to wish for nothing else. Days passed with little done outside but the gathering of sticks.

Then a hunter appeared, dragging a pile of meat on an elk hide. The boy went out and helped him with it as if an agreed division of labor had long been in place.

"Nice fire you have going there in my grate," the hunter said. The boy nodded, warming his hands by the fire as the hunter did.

They cooked elk steaks, watched the drip of grease. And when they had eaten the hunter produced a bottle of rye and filled cups made of wood and horn. The boy took a sip, but was more interested in the cup than its contents. It was more like a bowl, really; the wooden base was like a stump, with its roots cut to form a level standing base. And the wood at the upper edges where the horn vessel was enclosed was minutely carved into a mountain range.

"I don't just hunt," the man said. "Come to town with me tomorrow."

The man opened a sliding warehouse door to the smell of sawdust. He lit lanterns and showed the boy his wood working equipment.

"Mostly I make bowls," he said. "But there are other things."

The boy looked at walking canes and carved pistol grips—and a tiny village in an eggshell that could be viewed through a peephole. And bowls. Bowls that seemed to hold and incorporate the hands of those who held them. The boy mused as he touched polished surfaces everywhere, forsaking the world for the maps he found in wood grain. And the hunter knew he had an apprentice.

13.

The girl moved toward the places her painting revealed to her. She had put all that she wanted to keep of what she owned in a handcart, and, dressed in stout shoes and a broad hat, she moved from town to town, toward mountains. People streamed past her, headed in the opposite direction; she smiled at this—a refugee headed in the wrong direction.

She walked through mountains. She crossed forests and was ferried across rivers. And finally she came to a pass in a low chain of mountains that curved away from her to the north and south. Some travelers appearing there paused and spoke to her.

"Nothing ahead but a big prairie and a pass at the other side," a woman said. "No place to stop but an abandoned house in the middle, but there's a good well there. Good water."

The girl went on. Waving grass took hold of the land and the dusty ruts of the one road appeared; she felt herself relax for what seemed like the first time.

She had entered the prairie at daybreak and walked all day without seeing another traveler. When the sun was low in the sky her thoughts turned toward setting up camp. But just then she saw a shape ahead that seemed to stand in the road. It was the small house made of clay, the very one spoken of by the woman at the pass and by her mother long before.

The girl entered the house and straight away sat in a chair at a table, as if she had simply returned from one of many trips to garden or well. The silence around her gave way to crickets; she lit a candle which she found where she thought it should be. And by its light she straightened up the three rooms, dusting chairs and sweeping. She stood for much of the night looking at the baby's crib by the window that was almost in the road. The light of stars fell into it like milk with a blue tinge. She let her fingers trail over the white sheet that still covered the straw-filled mattress, and she followed the lines of dead vines that twined about the bars of the window. Finally she retreated to the bed in the other room, and slept.

14.

The young man set out from his own shop, headed west with a wagonload of bowls he had made. Asian markets had opened on the coast, and they paid handsomely for works they sent on to other lands. He went south first, and then worked his way north along the ocean shore. When all his wares were gone he paused for a day in a teeming city to rest and to eat well before heading east. He went to a restaurant built on a high street that faced the ocean, and as he sat waiting for his food he saw that the walls were painted. They were painted with vistas that seemed to hold no regard for what people usually wanted to see in such views; and when such things appeared, the wanting of them had changed in the course of looking. The man's food was delivered to him but it grew cold as he gazed at the walls all around. Who could have moved a brush like that without being overwhelmed by the world appearing? Surely memory could not hold such a thing, and desire alone could not conjure it. It was the pain of beauty he saw, uncommon but common to many shapes.

The waiter came and apologized for the distraction caused by the "scenery." He waved his hand in a gesture of mock appreciation, and offered to warm the man's food again.

Distracted, the man looked up at the waiter. "If the food was as remarkable as the scenery," he said, "it would not have cooled." Then he smiled, and the waiter, relieved, smiled as well. The man asked him about the artist and heard only that she had moved on. "Which way?" the man asked. "No telling," the waiter said. "Perhaps she's headed back to where she saw all of this," he added, turning to gaze at the images on the wall.

The man paid for his meal and left. And he went on, away from ocean waves. He made his way east, and finally the landscape began to look familiar, though he had no knowledge of having ever been present in it.

15.

The young woman heard the clink of traces and she stepped out into the road in her bare feet. She wore a long dress she had made from cloth acquired in trade; it was pale purple in color and she had sewn rough crystal beads to its hem. She looked eastward for some sign of a traveler, but she was looking the wrong way. Behind her a voice called out, softly. "You were not in the painting I saw, but now you are," the man said. The woman turned to him, already smiling because of the trick of direction, and when she saw him something in her leaped toward him.

"You will want water," she said, shading her eyes.

As she turned to begin drawing it the man called for her to wait. He brought her a cup of wood and horn, with mountains carved at its edges. She held it and gazed at its intricacies, and when she looked up his expression answered that it was what it seemed to be.

She took him in and cooked for him, running out at times to pull an onion from the garden or pinch leaves from herbs. They spoke of their travels into the night. And then they circled about the house, looking for the place each would sleep, and they circled until they returned to each other, smiling, settling down where they were.

They gardened and drew water for the infrequent travelers. The man had brought blanks of fine wood and new tools, and he had on his wagon a roll of paper he used to wrap bowls that were sold. So the woman painted, and wove bags of twisted grass to take the place of the paper she used. And the man carved.

16.

Scratches on a wooden calendar showed the woman's birthday was near, and the man had nothing to give her that was not already hers. She laughed when he asked her what she liked that she didn't have. She told him there was nothing she didn't have. And when he pressed her she laughed and said she wanted knowledge of what the hawk sees. She wanted colors that produced a reliable sound. And she wanted a bowl of shaved ice, dark with the juice of blackberries.

17.

Before sunrise the man packed a lunch of bread and hard cheese, and he drew water for his canteen. He left a note for the sleeping woman that said he would return soon with something she didn't have. And he set out for the north rim of the mountains. He rode the mule, free of its wagon-pulling chore, and in a large saddlebag he carried sawdust. He would use it to pack around the ice he hoped to find, and he would gather berries as he found them.

18.

The woman read the note and frowned, then rocked herself a while. She wished he had not gone. Not on this day, in particular, when she had planned to tell him of the new life on its way.

19.

The man reached the mountains in the early afternoon—later than he had anticipated. Cliffs rose above him and he turned the mule to follow the unrecognizable circle. When he had gone at least two miles he despaired of his task and pulled up, resolved to turn back for home. But just then he saw a white wall between mountain teeth. Ages of snow had slipped to a shaded cleft in the rock, and like a glacier it rode the inverted triangle and calved to melt water where it met the sun. So astonishing was the frozen structure before him, the man was not content to gather cold shards and pack them away. He tethered the mule loosely to a hank of grass and climbed the rock beside the ice.

At the top he paused, and he marveled to find the ice stretching like a road before him, a road headed north. He walked the rough surface and his shoes crunched with each step. He walked as if on a great pier that extended out into the tops of trees. He slowed when the ice began to slope downward and decided to turn back. But he slipped. He laughed at his clumsiness, and dug in with the edges of his shoes as best he could. But he slipped further and suddenly gathered speed. He was tumbling then, with spans of flight and impact, and then a long fall came in which he called out his love's name. Tree limbs broke his fall, but not so much that his leg was not snapped when he stopped in a jumble of rocks.

When he woke it was dark, and a cold wind was blowing. The man thought of his love, waiting for his return. He set himself the task of splinting his leg, keeping his thoughts apart from his body—as if he were a doctor tending to an unknown patient. When he could stand and walk with the aid of a stick, he approached the ice. He circled its edges, but everywhere its face was glassy and steep.

He turned then and looked at the land in which he found himself. It was nothing like the plain. Trees grew from cracks in rock, and cracked rock showed the work of present and long dead forests. Walking for a man with two good legs would have been hard going, but the smooth incline of ice left no choice. The man tucked his chin and set out, headed for the east pass. The rough terrain seemed to be matched by severity of weather: the temperature dropped as darkness came and gusts of wind made whips of low branches. Morning, though, found the man pressing on—distance and time already gone, already small in the face of a will to be true.

20.

There is a wide plain set in a bowl of mountains. A pass at the eastern boundary and a pass at the west allow travelers to cross, but the trail is seldom used. A single road—two ruts that gently rise and fall—cuts straight across. The only structure in the whole expanse is a house made of clay at the trail's mid point. A woman there makes her living drawing water for travelers. The house is set so close to the road that a baby in his crib, by the window facing the ruts, may reach out, unnoticed, and trail his fingers across the flanks of passing horses.